Ariadne, I Love You

"Ashley-Smith uses this eerie, ambiguous ghost story to explore the fraught relationship between artist and muse and the thin line between love and obsession . . . The result is multilayered, atmospheric, and thought-provoking."
—*Publishers Weekly*

"Sensual and deadly, enticingly sinister."
—*Aurealis Magazine, #141*

"*Ariadne, I Love You*, by J. Ashley-Smith, is my favorite kind of horror story: intimate, whip-smart, and relentless. The protagonist is in many ways a terrible human being: selfish, directionless, blind to the needs of others—and totally sympathetic, at least to this jaded reader. He is also doomed, which comes as no surprise. The mechanism of that doom is a surprise, though, and a delightfully awful one. More stories like this, please."
—Nathan Ballingrud, author of *North American Lake Monsters* and *Wounds: Six Stories from the Border of Hell*

"Ashley-Smith makes the reader feel like a sick voyeur in *Ariadne, I Love You*, as he takes us on a road trip through a diseased, obsessed, restless, haunted soul. Highly recommended."
—Kaaron Warren, winner of the Shirley Jackson Award

"J. Ashley-Smith has created a superbly written tale of love and haunted passion, with a poetic ambiance that leaves this reader both sympathetic and unsettled."
—Robert Hood, award-winning author of *Peripheral Visions: The Complete Ghost Stories*, and *Fragments of a Broken Land: Valarl Undead*

"Fallen-on-hard-times musician Jude has always loved Coreen, even when she was his best mate's girl, even after she was dead. But this is no conventional love story nor is it a conventional horror story. J. Ashley-Smith has an eye for the right precise detail that illuminates characters who seem to live and breathe well beyond the bounds of his evocative prose. *Ariadne, I Love You* is a powerful novella of enigmas and delusion and madness, of the lies we tell others and ourselves, and of the darkness at the heart of love. This is the kind of oblique, unsettling fiction I'm always looking for and too rarely find; I highly recommend it."
—Lynda E. Rucker, award-winning author of *The Moon Will Look Strange* and *You'll Know When You Get There*

"J. Ashley-Smith deftly blurs the lines between real and nightmare, love and obsession, in this haunting novella of aged rock stars, unrequited devotion, and the unassailable power that the past has over us. In here, guilt, grief, and regret leave an opening for worse things to tempt us in the buzzing darkness. You'll feel *Ariadne, I Love You* whether you want to or not."
—Simon Strantzas, author of *Nothing is Everything*

"A haunting tale of desire and madness and what might—or might not—be love. Ashley-Smith weaves a compelling story of music, bone, and nightmare."
—Angela Slatter, award-winning author of *All the Murmuring Bones*

"A nuanced and numinous rock 'n' roll Gothic about the distances—in time and space—that a broken heart will go to terrifyingly reassemble. You might begin J. Ashley-Smith's condensed riff on the abyss of student longing, artistic burnout and unresolved grief, on the train. You almost certainly will continue reading while stirring the pasta and eating it, and halfway through your meal you will look up from your second glass of wine and wonder where the hell you are."
—J.S. Breukelaar, author of *The Bridge*

"Ashley-Smith understands that ghost stories are, most importantly and at their core, about people, and with *Ariadne, I Love You*, he's crafted a haunting, ambiguous, confident and ghastly tale of eternal love."

—Keith Rosson, author of *Folk Songs For Trauma Surgeons*
and *The Mercy of the Tide*

Previous Praise for
The Attic Tragedy

"Ashley-Smith debuts with a gorgeous, melancholy coming-of-age novella about girlhood and ghosts.... This eerie, ethereal tale marks Ashley-Smith as a writer to watch."

—Publishers Weekly

"A beautifully written book about desire, pain, and loss, haunted by glimmerings of the supernatural. *The Attic Tragedy* manages to do more by intimation and suggestion with its fifty-three pages than most novels manage to accomplish over their several hundred."

—Brian Evenson, author of *Song for the Unraveling of the World*

"*The Attic Tragedy* is full of heart and darkness, both endearing and terrifying. These pages open like a raw wound. You don't read this story. It bleeds into you, and it leaves a scar on the way in."

—Sarah Read, Bram Stoker Award® winning author of
The Bone Weaver's Orchard and *Out of Water*

"Softly shrouded in smoke and shadow, Ashley-Smith's *The Attic Tragedy* cuts close to the bone. Startling, pointed, and powerful."

—Lee Murray, Bram Stoker Award® winning author of
Grotesque: Monster Stories and *Into the Ashes*

Also by J. Ashley-Smith

THE ATTIC TRAGEDY

Ariadne, I LOVE YOU

a novella by

J. ASHLEY-SMITH

Meerkat Press
Asheville

ISBN-13: 978-1-946154-50-7 (Paperback)
ISBN-13 978-1-946154-51-4 (eBook)

Book cover and interior design by Tricia Reeks

Printed in the United States of America

Published in the United States of America by
Meerkat Press, LLC, Asheville, NC
www.meerkatpress.com

To those dead dreams
and the dear friends who dreamed them.

1

The ghost of the engine still roared in my ears as I popped the car door, swung my legs to the ground. From the gully below, the chimes of bellbirds echoed the tantrum of clunks and pings beneath the bonnet. I staggered, stretched, felt my knees creak. Reached back in to grab my cigs. That first blue-gray exhalation was pure reverence and I savored it, stood with one hand on the open door, not ready to commit to the fresh air, the open sky, the back-arse-of-nowhere vibe.

The abandoned train carriage was a dreary beige, with smoky windows, blank and hollow. Beyond its weathered deck and the turning circle of dust and weeds, the bristling wilderness stretched in all directions to infinity. Proper bleak.

"Mate, it's yours," Ben had said. "You can stay there till your show, or as long as you need."

Magnanimous bastard. Like I had a choice.

I tossed the butt and went looking for the key. The sun was long down and my denim jacket was no protection against the prickling cold. Chill gusts from the gully made the dry leaves rattle like a thousand tiny bones.

The key was in a rusty can below the deck, just as Ben had said. It had a plastic tag and a handwritten label. *Her* handwriting. The back of my head tingled like I was being watched, and I turned around quickly to catch—I don't know what—some movement. But there was nothing. Only the gentle marionette gestures of branches, the soughing of leaves like the ocean in a seashell.

Up the half-rotten stairs and onto the deck, I found double doors laced with cobwebs, took out the key and felt my heart tumble again over Coreen's writing on the tag. The door was jammed, so I shouldered it and stumbled into the carriage. The smell of dead air struck me at once—not damp, as I'd expected, but old and absent, the smell of forgotten things. Mildew bloomed in the double-glazed windows, distorting the view and dimming what remained of the daylight.

I found the old fuse box, decorated with stickers of rainbows and unicorns that half-glittered as I pulled it open. Inside were more keys with more handwritten tags and a ring binder with instructions for visitors. I flicked through the pages: water tank, gas cooker, pit toilet, air bed, *flick, flick, flick*. I could sort all that out later. I stepped through the bead curtain into the carriage's main compartment.

The lounge was scattered with the detritus of family life. A game of Hungry Hippos, unfinished on the carpet. Drawing paper on the coffee table, big shapes scrawled in brightly colored crayon. A neat stack of line drawings in black felt tip—a crow, a lizard, an animal that might have been a wombat. On the arm of the couch, a pile of books: *Tender is the Night*; *The Beautiful and Damned*; Nietzsche's *Birth of Tragedy*. Coreen's old postgraduate bedfellows.

There wasn't much to the "master bedroom." A deflated airbed gathering dust and clumps of hair. A coil of fly-paper dangling from a blackened air vent. A shabby wicker chair piled with old music magazines. Hardly the fucking Ritz. And the air, so still and close. I was on my way to throw open the back door when something above the bed caught my eye.

The photo was set in a handmade frame of warped bushwood. A selfie of them both, looking just how I remembered. Ben, with his gawky, boyish face, his ginger mop and trademark newsreader specs. And *her*, Coreen, with her pale skin and chaos of black hair, her arm off to one side holding the camera, mouth twisted into that half-frown I knew to be a grin. It must have been taken only a couple of years after they left London, because they were still young. Before kids. Before—

It was a candid shot, perfectly captured. A private moment of intimacy between two people very much in love.

I put up my hand, laid it over the picture, cutting off Ben. Even through the lens of the camera in her hand, even out of that frozen instant and across the years that separated us, there she was. Her fierce blue eyes fixed on mine.

2

"She told me she wanted a cat," Ben said. We were in the kitchen of his Newtown terrace. The windows were steamed. Ben's glasses, too. He reached into the pot with a slotted spoon and teased out a quill of pasta, tested it, pulled a face.

I was perched on a stool at the breakfast bar, beneath a rack of dangling pans. Ben uncorked another red, raised his eyebrows and waved the bottle in my direction. I nodded and knocked back what was in my glass, held it out for him to fill.

"And she banged on and on about it, wouldn't let it go. You know what kids are like."

"I can imagine," I said, but was only half listening. Since I arrived that afternoon, Ben had talked about nothing but parenthood, the quirks and foibles of this or that offspring. I stifled a yawn between pressed lips, washed it down with another glug of red.

"Anyway, I was this close to going down the shelter and picking one out, when I twigged: it wasn't a pet she wanted, it was a cadaver." Ben tasted the sauce, started laying out bowls for us and the girls. "I said no, of course. You've got to draw the line somewhere."

"Is this all since . . ." I couldn't bring myself to say it. We hadn't yet spoken about Coreen.

Ben shook his head. "Nah, Margot's pretty much always been

a dark one; 'scientific,' she'd call it. The bones thing started with a wombat skull she found last time we were down the train. This kitchen's been like a mortician's lab ever since. We've had birds, rats, lizards, all stretched out on the chopping board to be skinned and dissected, the bones boiled clean. I'm not even sure they're all dead when she finds them."

I pulled a face, hoping it conveyed the expected emotion. I'd caught a glimpse of Margot's room on my last piss stop. The velvety purple walls, the gleaming bell jars, the displays of mounted animal skeletons and antique taxidermy. It was more like a ghoulish private museum than an eight-year old's bedroom.

"Couple of months after I shut it down, she came home with something in a plastic bag. It stank, and flies were buzzing." Ben shook his head again. "Our neighbor's cat had been hit by a car and Margot scooped it out of the gutter and brought it home. Christ, what a mess! I had to help her disembowel it, and the bloody thing was so big we had to go down the hardware store for an industrial-size pot."

I glanced over Ben's shoulder at the pot on the stove, wisps of vapor curling from the rim.

"The kitchen stank for weeks. And I still can't look the Habibis in the eye."

"Is dinner *ever* going to be ready?"

Peg erupted into the kitchen, a five-year-old whirlwind of strawberry-blonde hair and rainbow tie-dye. She seemed to explode out of another dimension, where standing still was a capital crime and every object on the floor a stepping-stone. I scooped up my bag and put it on the stool beside me.

"Just serving now," said Ben. "Go tell your sister."

Ben laid the table and invited me to sit, spooned pasta and sauce into the bowls, garnished all but one with some chopped green stuff. He was just tearing the bread when Peg burst back in, Margot walking stiffly behind her.

My heart stopped when I looked up and I prickled all over, like I was seeing a ghost.

Margot was the mirror image of her mother, but at the same time not like her at all—a waxwork, both identical and wrong. Her hair was the same midnight black, but unlike Coreen's it hung in a straight, neat bob. Her skin had the same powdery whiteness, but on Margot it looked ashen, almost consumptive. And the thought of Coreen in a starched white blouse and old-style charcoal pinafore was absurd.

In two details, though, she was completely identical, and it was these that held me dangling over the pit in my own stomach. Her mouth was pulled down at the edges in a frown that I knew would express both amusement and displeasure. And her eyes—

I realized I was staring and flicked my gaze around the walls, as though Margot was just one piece in a gallery full of other, more diverting exhibits.

She looked at me without interest.

"You must be the one from Daddy's band," she said.

I ignored the slight, forced a smile. "The one and only," I said. "I've known your dad since back in the day."

"His name is Jude, Margot," Ben said. "Peg. Fork."

Peg's head was tilted to one side as she shoveled pasta into her mouth by the handful. Her face, from cheek to chin, was slick with smears of bright red sauce. She looked at me and grinned, her wide-open mouth a grinder of tumbling, half-chewed food.

"I brought the old album." I turned to Ben, though it was for Margot's benefit that I said it; for some reason I couldn't bring myself to look at her. "Thought it might be good for a listen."

"Yay yay yay!" Peg went manic. She was out of her seat, stomping and jumping around the chair, food flying as she yelled. "The album! The album! Let's listen to Daddy's album!"

"You still with Mack?" Ben asked.

"Pretty much," I said, protecting my glass from Peg's flailing. "He crawled out of the woodwork fast enough when this show came up. Said he'd be over in a week or two, to crack the whip, take his cut."

"You got anything on the way?"

"Nothing new. Though Mack was pushing for a *Best Of* to tie in with the show." I shrugged. "Not going to happen now, unless he plans to burn them himself."

Ben laughed, topped up my glass.

"I enjoyed your last one," he said. "Couple of nice little numbers. Not a patch on *Troubled Heart*, mind. But you must've known that was a one-off; pure bloody magic from go to whoa. What was the single again?"

"'Baby, Leave Your Man,'" I said, and felt my heart pound to speak those words aloud in front of Ben. "That was the big one."

"With the harmonies? Bloody magic that one."

Peg had forgotten about dinner, twirled round and round the table like a runaway drill. It made me tense and giddy, but Ben didn't seem to notice. Margot watched her sister without interest, lifting penne to her mouth one quill at a time.

After dinner, I snuck off to the lounge while Ben and Margot did the washing up. I sat back on the faded leather couch, knocked back more wine, picked a tune on Ben's old acoustic. I was thinking of Coreen and didn't notice what I was playing until I felt the pull in my chest, the crack in my throat. I would have stopped, but Peg joined me then with a toy bongo, marched, yelling, round the living room, pounding the drum not quite in time to the music. I couldn't bring myself to sing.

When Ben came in at last, I was knelt by the stereo, sticking on the CD. He picked up the case, had a laugh at the photo. The Böring Straights. Me and Ben and the others from the old band, all done up in black-and-white suits, half corporate, half Reservoir Dogs, trying way too hard to look rock'n'roll.

Ben tossed back the case and I looked down at it, realized I was stalling until Margot was in the room. I looked at my younger self, felt a twinge of something that might have been sadness, might have been just the hollow feeling of lost time.

I pushed play, cranked the volume. The opening bars of "I Wanna Be Incorporated" blasted out and Peg went nuts, full-on moshing round the room. Ben lay back in an easy chair, eyes closed, an almost-grin tweaking the edge of his mouth. I stretched along the couch with my feet up, half caught in the mistakes I'd obsessed over since the album was first pressed, half checking the others' reactions. Margot was perched on the pouf in the corner with an unreadable expression.

As each song juddered to a stop or rang out in a squall of feedback, I found I was holding my breath, my right hand clenched into a fist. And my mind was clenched just as tight, second-guessing, as each new song started, what Margot would like about it. Or dislike. Trying to gauge, from the smallest reactions, what her feelings were for this thing I had created. Or whether she had feelings for it at all.

When she got up in the middle and left, I felt as though part of me had broken.

3

Always wake in terror. Powerless, cold, alone. Always that lingering smell, of woodsmoke and moss. The weight of cold rock.

Some nights I feel I'm buried alive. Wake up screaming, clawing dirt from my throat. There is the weight of the rocks and the smell that lingers even after I wake. I can smell it in the room. As though He is in the room.

I know he is still there. I can feel him inside me. Inside my head. He whispers pain, the pressure that throbs like a living thing, so deep in my skull I can't reach. Always worse after sleep. Always wake in fear and pain, pulling at my hair so I won't hear him whisper, won't feel what's left behind. The swelling black seed he planted inside me.

Always in the dream he is indistinct. As vague as woodsmoke, with the smell of deep age and moss. A smell of both life and death. He frightens me, yet I long for him. And the longing frightens me more. He is there in that place, part of it even. No, he is not there—He is the Place. And the Place is Him.

I have been chosen. I am his one.

Through pain he speaks. "You are mine," he says. "And forever more shall be." The pain is his longing, a cord stretched to snapping by distance. By absence. His pain will be mine until I return, until he pulls me back to the place that is him. And there he will take from me all that I am. All but the bones.

The smell is still with me when I wake. I scrub and scrub until my skin is raw and my hair comes out in clumps. But nothing can make it go away.

Nothing can make it go away.

4

That first night at the train I slept in the car.

It got dark quickly, too dark for me to read Coreen's instructions, too dark to find a lamp even. The bed was unpumped, I hadn't any water, hadn't set up the stove or the toilet, didn't know where to lay my hands on anything I could use for anything.

I took the photo with me. Pulled it down off the wall and out of the frame, folded it in half with Ben on the back. I had to break the frame to get it out, but who was to know? Ben was in no rush to come back here. And Coreen—

Even with the passenger seat flipped all the way back, it wasn't much of a bed. I wrapped myself in my jacket, ate the remains of a chocolate bar I'd bought on the way, washed it down with a bottle of red. I'd maxed out my last credit card on a crate of wine and a case of cigs, my only supplies—and the only reason I was camped out in bumfuck nowhere, instead of holed up at the Sydney Hilton. I smoked one after another, holding the picture of Coreen. She looked into me like she could read my mind, all those secrets I thought I'd left buried.

If I slept at all it didn't feel like it. I couldn't get comfortable and the night cold settled deep in my bones. I left the engine running and cranked up the heat, but the wine left me parched and restless. What shreds of sleep I did snatch were tangled with dreams from some halfway place. Growls, barks, rustles and scrapes—the unearthly sounds came at one moment from the trees, the next from the gully, once from right outside the car. I switched the headlights on full beam, but the tungsten brightness only made the dark all the darker, and alive with unknowable things. When at last I did pass out, I was dragged awake by the mockery of kookaburras. My eyes were swollen and sore, the trees in the gully silhouetted against a bruised dawn.

I got out of the car and stomped around to warm up. My hands were shaking from the cold. I needed coffee and water and hot food and had none of those things, so lit a cig instead, coughed so long and hard I almost spewed.

I thought I remembered a thing or two from Coreen's instructions, so lugged the two-burner stove onto the deck, rummaged among rusty tools until I found a wrench to hook it to the gas. I dug out a tin mug, a jar of Nescafé, and a Tupperware crusted shut with hardened sugar. I took a jerry can round to the water tank, soaked my sleeves and my cig, dragged the sloshing can back to the deck to fill the kettle and a glass. The water was the color of piss and alive with wriggling things.

I tossed it, sank down to the deck, let my head fall into my hands.

No doubt Ben would have everything up and running by now. Ben would have coffee on the stove and bacon in the pan. Ben would have the bed pumped, the fire lit, the water clean. Fucking Ben. He cast a shadow so long that, even here, a thousand-and-one miles from anywhere, he made me feel like a feckless nobody.

Which pretty well summed up our history to this moment.

I met Ben on the first day of university. I'd skipped the lecture, gone straight to the bar, and there he was: a ginger beanpole in glasses, skinny jeans and a *Goo* T-shirt, clutching a pint of Guinness with his elbow stuck out like he'd broken something. I was a teenage misfit, with a stickered guitar case in my hand and a copy of *Thus Spoke Zarathustra* in my pocket. Dyed black hair, black combat boots, and a too-big black trench coat with the sleeves rolled up. I'd chosen philosophy for all the obvious reasons: innate laziness and a complete lack of skill or ambition for anything other than music. I didn't see the point in a degree, had no interest in getting a job, and only went to university to meet other losers, start a deadly band and become a rock star. And this lanky goon looked perfect—my first recruit.

I made some remark about his tee and we got talking, about Sonic Youth, about Mudhoney, about the death of Kurt Cobain. Ben knew his shit. In fact, when it came to music, he was a walking encyclopedia.

I can still remember the offhand, almost innocent way he belittled me that first day. We'd been in the bar all morning and were proper tanked. The conversation had turned from music to philosophy. When I say "conversation," what I mean is that Ben was off on one, ranting about this and that with supporting gesticulations of his ungainly limbs.

". . . of course, after Derrida it's impossible to take anything at face value. I mean, no matter what you might have believed, or *thought* you believed, once you go back and look at it in miniature, *deconstruct* it, then . . ."

I remember how pummeled I felt by his intellect, and the feeling that I'd nothing of value to contribute. I remember nodding, drinking, smoking cig after cig, barely following what he was saying. But I didn't want to look stupid, and was mad keen to impress him. So I waited for him to draw breath, then jumped in.

"But what about Nietzsche? The superman?"

"Exactly!" He said, with a snap of his fingers. "That's precisely the kind of rubbish Derrida was talking about! Although, you hardly need to deconstruct Nietzsche to see what a lot of drivel he was spouting. I mean, who even *reads* that nonsense these days? Goths. Nazis. Teenage serial killers."

I remember how my coat felt heavy with that old copy of *Zarathustra*, how my face flushed with embarrassment.

Fucking Ben.

#

The sun was almost above the tree line, but I was no closer to meeting my basic physiological needs. What I *had* achieved, slumped on the edge of the deck, was to assemble an impressive collection of cigarette butts. When I stubbed out my last, I knew it was time to get it together; if only to stand up and grab another pack of cigs from the case.

The instructions were on the floor of the carriage, where I'd left them. I took them back to butt city and began to read.

The water from the tank is fine to drink, if you're not precious about the color (that's right, Princess. I'm talking to you!). No need to boil. In summer it's full of wrigglers, so use the water filter. If you're dying of starvation, you can skip the filter and enjoy some bonus protein. Yum!

I ran my fingers over the words, hearing Coreen's voice. I smiled in spite of myself and felt again that deep ache. If I closed my eyes, I could almost see her funny mouth, her wonky eyebrows. It hurt.

I went back into the train and dug around until I found the filter jug, filled it from the can and searched the shelves for food. I found enough tins to last me through the apocalypse, but settled on beans and a half-empty bottle of lime cordial, took them out to the deck just as the water finished trickling through the filter. I filled the kettle, filled a glass. The water was bitter, had a faintly metallic aftertaste, but wasn't so bad. I knocked back another glass, with cordial this time, felt it rinse away the carpet on my tongue. I heated the beans, ate them straight from the pan, washed the lot down with two cups of sweet, black coffee. I let my legs dangle from the deck, swinging idly as I savored the after-meal smoke.

Dig out Jimmy's Thunder Box. Unless you're the village idiot (in which case, what the fuck are you doing in my train, Cletus!) you can work out how to put this together. The Thunder Box will just about fit over the hole in the dunny. Make sure you get the seals right or you'll find yourself in a sticky situation (and there's no bath here, if you follow my drift).

Out beyond the end of the train was a structure of wood and tin. The outhouse. I kicked away the rock that held the door shut, let it creak open. The inventory: a dusty roll of toilet paper; the desiccated turds of some unspecified marsupial; a cockroach skittering through the debris of neglect.

I let the door hang and stepped back out to the edge of the gully. The ground there fell away to a snake nest of rocks and felled eucalypts, to tangles of native creeper. Below and beyond were layer upon layer of darkening green. A cold gust whispered from the gully, made me shiver. Again there was that unpleasant tingle, the sense of being watched. I thought I saw movement within the trees, but though I strained to make it out I didn't see it again.

Pump for the bed is in That Seventies Cupboard and the sheets, blankets etc are in the plastic tubs by the back door. Make sure you close them when you're done as these make great RAT NESTS! . . . Coffee beans, grinder and stovetop espresso pot are beside the fire extinguisher: break glass in case of emergency! . . . Love fire? You got it! There's wood under the deck and a leaning tower of papers in the old kitchen. Just don't burn down my fucking train!

It took most of the day, but I worked through those instructions page by page. It'd been so long since I last saw Coreen, last spoke to her, but there she was on every line. Her words. Her voice.

As I pumped and made the bed, set up the toilet, the kitchen, foraged in the cupboards for warm clothes, blankets, lamps, I felt she was right there with me, leading me through it, guiding me, and all the while taking the piss. It made me feel happy, in a way. The way a phantom limb might make you feel happy if you'd lost a leg.

Until you tried to scratch it, that is.

Or walk.

5

I fell in love with Coreen the moment I met her.

My train had pulled into London that afternoon and Ben and I had been out on the piss since he got off work. It was three years since uni, two since The Böring Straights crashed and burned.

Ben had an upstairs maisonette in Brixton, a job in the A&R team at Parlophone, and an Australian girlfriend that he just would not shut up about. He and Coreen lived together with a Taiwanese economics student, Albert, who rented the spare room. I'd come to London to seek my fortune, with nothing but a change of clothes and a CD Walkman, my trusty acoustic in a case held together by stickers and an old belt. Ben told me I could crash a few nights until I got settled.

I was on the couch, nursing one of the cans of Red Stripe we'd picked up on the way home. Ben was on his knees by the stereo, rummaging among the cascade of unboxed CDs. The door slammed below and someone tramped up the stairs. I figured it was Albert, who'd vanished with a polite nod when we first got in, crashing and shouting, disruptively drunk. A bag slammed against the couch behind me.

"Judas Iscariot, I presume?"

"Oh, hey babe," said Ben, turning from his search. "Yeah,

this is Jude." He made a half-hearted gesture, "Jude—Coreen, Coreen—Jude."

Coreen dropped down on the other end of the couch, nodded toward the cans, gave me a look. "You keeping all those for yourself, are you?"

I tried to speak, but all that came out was a mumble.

"Fuck me, Ben," said Coreen, reaching between my feet and grabbing a can. "You said he was withdrawn, not bloody catatonic."

Coreen leaned over to the coffee table, an old trunk overflowing with newspapers and tattered copies of Melody Maker, NME, helped herself to one of my cigs. She lit it without flourish and sat back, blowing smoke in a mean upward plume, worrying the filter with her sharp white thumb. She'd come straight from work and was wearing an unflattering black T-shirt with the venue's logo. I watched her pop the can of Stripe, watched her Adam's apple bob as she drank. Black hair spilled from a scrappy topknot, framing that pale face on which the most prominent features were cold blue eyes and a mouth that did not smile, only frowned to greater or lesser degrees. The bangles on her arm tinkled cheaply with every drag she took.

I realized I was staring so took a sudden interest in my beer can, lit another cig to look busy.

Ben had found what he was looking for, some band he was gunning to sign, all edgy guitars and mechanical beats, sharp angles, strangled vocals. He hit play, came over to Coreen and leaned in to kiss her cheek.

"Shit, babe. Not this, please," she said, turning away. "I've been hammered by this crap all night and just need something . . .else. Have you got nothing with a bit of fucking *heart*?"

Ben looked confused, started to speak but changed his mind, got back down on his knees by the CD stack.

"I've maybe got something," I said, and passed over the CD

I'd bought in Camden that afternoon. *Sweetheart of the Rodeo* by the Byrds.

Coreen snatched it and drew her feet up onto the couch, scrutinized the cover. She chewed her cuticles, cigarette resting against her cheek. She shrugged, tossed the CD over to Ben who fumbled the catch, looked at the cover with a raised eyebrow, slid the CD into the tray.

My heart was pounding. I couldn't have felt any more exposed if I'd been sitting there naked. The opening bars of "You Ain't Going Nowhere" shuffled and twanged from the speakers and I cringed; why had I given her *this*? I was holding my breath, muscles tensed, sick with shame at the putdown I knew was coming.

But it never did. Coreen took a long swig from her can, closed her eyes. The chorus swelled, layer upon layer of harmonies so lush they would have melted me at any other time. I hardly dared look up, but stole a glance, saw Coreen nodding minutely. I began to relax, pulled myself another can, tossed one to Ben.

"So, Country Joe," said Coreen, turning to face me. "Spill. Tell me what you're thinking."

And, with that, set the stage for one of the best nights of my life.

We smashed the beers in no time and Coreen sent Ben out into the night for more booze. We talked music and poetry and passion, magical babble that went in one ear and out the other I was so drunk; buoyant, like some ecstatic cloud, just watching her mouth move, her eyes gleam. She ranted about opera, broke into a (dreadful) aria from *The Valkyrie*, raved about her PhD—*Tragic Optimist: semblance and intoxication in the life of Zelda Fitzgerald*—about the artist's muse and the cost to those women who'd carried it, about Nietzsche's pessimism and his first book, *The Birth of Tragedy out of the Spirit of Music*.

"We're all fucked, is pretty much what he's saying. Life is a meaningless horror and we know it but we pretend we don't so as not to just fucking top ourselves."

"Cheery", I said.

"Absolutely not," she said. "And that's the point! Groundless optimism, happiness, that's all just us pretending everything's okay, that we're not just pointless specks of nothing hurtling through infinite empty space. It's *tragedy* that lets us wake up to the horror without being destroyed by it."

Coreen reached over, shook out the last cigarette from my pack, lit it, took a long drag and passed it over. She raised her eyebrows and two fingers. *Twos-up?* I nodded, took a drag and passed it back.

"See," she went on, pausing to return the cig. "In tragedy—the old Greek kind anyway—you've got these two forces pulling against each other. On the one side you've got Apollo: he's the words, the drama, the *structure* in everything; he's what makes us distinct, what makes me *me* and you *you*. And then there's Dionysus: the chorus, the music; he's ecstasy and intoxication; this blind, primordial energy pushing up from the earth, the life in everything, and the death as well. You and me, Judy: Dionysus is our man. Without him a poem's just a string of words, and a melody's only notes. Like the best music, or great sex, Dionysus breaks down the barriers between us, makes us one again."

I shifted uncomfortably. As her monologue intensified, Coreen had leaned in closer. Her proximity, her fervor—not to mention the talk of sex—tingled in my groin like an electric current. I crossed my legs.

"In a way, the whole thing's about sex—not that Nietzsche would have said so. On the one hand, *The Birth of Tragedy* is an ode to how much he wanted to bum Wagner, the hard-on he got for that Wagnerian tragic ideal. On the other ... Well, Nietzsche gave the manuscript to Cosima, Wagner's wife, for her birthday. Kind of a roundabout way to proposition a little extramarital nookie. It failed, of course—this *is* Nietzsche we're talking about."

Coreen took a long last drag on the cig, burning it right down to the filter. She reached forward, dropped the remains into the Greene King ashtray at her feet.

"He went full-on bonkers before he died," she said. "Did you know that? Had a stroke, went crackers and sat up writing letters to people he'd not seen in years. His madness letters, they called them; the *Wahnbriefe*. He wrote one to Cosima, some cryptic shit he'd been simmering on for years, no doubt. Just four words: 'Ariadne, I love you.' That must have got her thinking."

"You know," I said, "I don't know what Ben's told you, but I'm really not that into Nietzsche."

Coreen gave me a look, cocked an eyebrow. "Right-o, Judy," she said. "Whatever you say."

She leaned in toward me then, until her mouth was beside my ear. I could feel the warmth of her breath on my neck and the smell that came off her, both sweet and faintly tart. My fists clenched in my lap, heart skipping so hard I thought I'd spew.

"I know when you're lying to me, Judy," she whispered, prodding my chest with a bony finger. "I *see* you. I don't give a shit what you like or don't like, only don't fucking lie to me."

I pulled back, met her eyes. I was confused, afraid even; I couldn't understand what she was trying to tell me. She looked right into me, the faintest pull of a frown on her lips. That look crackled. Seconds dilated.

The door slammed below and the moment burst. Coreen laughed.

Ben came into the room, grinning, weighed down by plastic bags. "What'd I miss?" he said.

On the table he laid out cigs, more Stripe, four cans of Red Bull and a bottle of vodka. It wasn't long before the guitars came out and we were plowing through half-baked covers of yesterday's classics: "Wild Horses" and "Son of a Preacher Man" and "Blowin' in the Wind." Coreen's singing voice was pig-awful, but she made up in spirit what she lacked in ability. It was a magical time, the three of us like that. One we would never reclaim.

Albert returned sometime after midnight and both Ben and Coreen tried to persuade him—with much childish, drunken cajoling—to join the party. Albert declined, backing into his room with apologetic nods. He didn't come out again until the morning, but couldn't have slept a wink for the noise we made.

The night didn't end so much as collapse. I woke up on the floor in a pool of spilled beer and ash. Coreen and Ben lay in a heap on the couch.

I knew then that I could never leave. And that she and I were meant to be.

6

Night. The sky a blue-black dome, untinged by the orange glow of the city, unbroken by any risen moon. Down in the gully, black silhouettes strained against a deeper darkness, blacker than black. Country dark.

I didn't like it. It felt bottomless. It looked back at me.

I was slumped in a camp chair by the gully's edge, a mug of red in one hand, Coreen's copy of *The Birth of Tragedy* open, unread, in my lap. An unlit head-lamp dangled from the chair's arm. I didn't like the dark, but the light was worse, made the world small, stifling, cast shadows that moved among the trees. I lit one cig with another, the orange glow tracing arcs as I raised hand to mouth and back again. I couldn't see the picture of Coreen, but could feel it against my palm. I caressed it with my thumb, the tiny bumps and folds like imperfections on bare skin.

I should have been practicing. The show was barely a week away and I was drunk in the dark, smoking myself to death, five-hundred miles or more from the venue. I should have gone to the car to grab my acoustic, sat out here in the dark and worked on my set. But my acoustic wasn't in the car. It was up in the window of Happy Hockers, Darlinghurst, where I'd cashed it in for three hundred and fifty dollars; a tenth of its real value. I'd get it back—of course I would. When Mack arrived in Sydney, we'd go straight over there and buy it out. Then the practice would really start. But until then I was in free-fall.

Just ten years ago I'd been on top of the world, cresting the alt-country wave that washed through the early Noughties. My second band, The Ride Me Highs, signed a four-album deal with Rough Trade, licensed to a Nashville major. Our first album was a critical smash, the second went gold in the US. We toured Europe with Wilco, the States with Son Volt, headlined in Japan, then back to the UK to do it all over again. When we weren't touring or in the studio, I was playing sessions, flogging songs to Country royalty. My mojo was un-fucking-breakable; I knocked out heartbreaker after heartbreaker.

But then it all turned to shit. The magic that powered those first years fizzled. I looked for it in any bottle to hand, but it was never there. No golden ticket, just another rock'n'roll cliché. What a joke. I got too pissed to write, too pissed to play, then the fucking band went and *fired* me. Fired *me*! I woke up one day in a Glasgow townhouse; I'd been drunk for three years, shacked up with the last of the great Coreen lookalikes, a blue-eyed black-haired Goth chick half my age. Next I knew, I was at Glasgow Central, about to step in front of a train, but I bottled at the last minute and got on instead, slunk back home to Mum.

I figured I'd never hear from our manager again. Hiding out in my childhood home, my life had become a loop of insomniac nights and unconscious days, of booze and sadness baths and boundless, insatiable loneliness. But there was Mack, on the phone, years later, telling me to scrub up and get ready for a comeback tour. No band, no baggage. Just me and a guitar and a fistful of alt-country hits.

He was exaggerating, of course. *Troubled Heart* had been Triple J's album of the whatever ten years ago and some bright spark had sold Mack on the idea of a retrospective gig. The "tour" was a one-off solo show at the Sydney Enmore, with supports to be arranged. Hardly worth getting out of bed for.

Only it was in Australia. And Australia meant Coreen.

I'd not seen her in ten years or more, but the old wound still sang. Some part of me still nursed the memory, understood that whatever magic I'd channeled at my peak had her as its source. Even in my decline the ghost of her lingered, animating every blue-eyed, black-haired lookalike who shared my bed. The thought of seeing her again was enough to lead me back to the guitar, to let those old songs come falling out, scratchy at first, uneasy, but familiar, and somehow better than I remembered them. With the promise of Coreen before me, the music was flowing again and I couldn't wait for the show to come around. A month ahead of Mack's schedule, I tapped my mum for cash and hopped on a plane. I didn't tell anyone I was coming. I wanted it to be a surprise.

I found out Coreen was dead the day I touched down in Sydney. I emailed to say I'd arrived, what I was doing, that we should catch up. My message bounced straight back with an out-of-office set up by Ben. He replied to me himself just a few minutes later, told me the news, said it was great to hear from me, that I should come round and see them some time. Him and the girls.

The news sank deep inside me, like a secret tied to a heavy stone. It came to rest on some abysmal ledge and lay there, emitting wave after wave of indistinct pain. I floated around Sydney like a ghost, blowing cash I didn't have on hotels and expensive meals, on boozing and taxis and drinks-are-on-me. Within a fortnight, I'd maxed out four credit cards, spent close on twenty thousand dollars I didn't have and couldn't possibly repay. It was only then, once my bridges were all burned, that I truly began to feel her loss, to see the pointlessness of everything I'd done, and was doing, without her to do it for.

⌗

The moon was just beginning to peek through the trees, but the gully below was still in total darkness. Something skittered nearby, some sharp-nailed creature scaling a eucalypt trunk. I couldn't see it, but I heard its progress, the gruff shout as it paused between boughs. My heart flip-flopped, began to race, but the instinct to run screaming was dulled by the booze. I clicked on the head-lamp and swung the beam up toward the sound.

Where the bough met the trunk, two diamonds shone then disappeared as the light went past. I moved it back, held it steady. The eyes were still there, glinting, frozen, a possum clinging motionless to the bark, pretending like mad that it didn't exist.

"Don't worry, mate," I slurred. "I'm not gonna eatcha."

I tossed the head-lamp down beside me. The beam lurched, then winked out as the battery casing popped open on a rock. Time for bed.

"G'night," I said, pushing against the arms of the camp chair. "G'night, li'l matey."

But I was too shit-faced to stand.

I went cross-eyed, collapsed back into the chair, stared down into the gully, past the outlines of trees too faint to be certain, past unknowable silhouettes, past all the different shades of black to that deeper black beneath everything, a black so deep I felt myself sink into it.

At first, I thought I was seeing things. But when I blinked, it was still there. Only closer. The small, blue-white light hovered eerily, darting this way and that, as though searching for something, flickering as it vanished and reappeared from within the trees.

The light twisted and turned in a convoluted dance, making its way up the gully. Straight toward me.

7

I crashed on the couch in that Brixton flat for weeks, made myself a nest in the corner and burrowed in like a rodent. It took on my shape, my smell.

Ben was too polite to say anything, although I could tell it bothered him. Every few days he'd pluck up the nerve to ask how my job search was going, my hunt for a place to live. Each time the answer was the same: "Mate, I'm looking. There's just *nothing* out there." Then I'd cadge a cig, get back to playing guitar, watching TV.

Each morning, the sound of Ben in the shower would patter at the edge of consciousness, a bit of unwelcome reality that insinuated itself into my dream world. I'd half wake to hear him in the kitchen, kettle boiling, toast popping, the clatter of cutlery on a plate. I'd fall back to sleep to the rustle of the newspaper, the crunch of toast, woken briefly by the dull bang of the front door. The whisper of socks on carpet, as Albert tiptoed from his room and down the stairs and out, barely made me stir.

Coreen, I knew, was awake, but would lounge in bed for another hour or so before heading to the shower. When I heard the kettle boil the second time, I'd rouse myself—that is, move my feet from the couch to the floor—and, still wrapped in the same unwashed duvet, spark up while Coreen made tea. We'd sit there together, sipping tea, smoking Ben's cigs, talking shit. Eventually, she'd drag herself up and into the bedroom to slog away at her thesis for an hour or two. I'd play guitar and smoke, maybe make another cup of tea. Some mornings I had a shower. After lunch, we'd watch TV until it was time for Coreen to go to work. If there was anything good on, I'd watch right through until Albert got back from uni and shut himself in his room. Other days I'd play guitar, or read whatever Coreen had left lying around the coffee table.

By the time Ben returned of an evening, the flat would reek like a smokehouse. We'd go to the pub on the corner, or the gig of some young hopefuls Ben was cultivating. When Coreen got back from work each night, Ben was turning in, and she and I would sit up and drink and talk until late. After she crashed, I'd lie awake, picking at Ben's unplugged Gibson or watching whatever crap was on TV.

And so the days revolved.

I knew Ben was getting ratty. I could hear him clucking and tutting in the mornings when he got ready for work, heard the muffled arguments when their bedroom door was closed.

When Albert moved out it was like destiny. I scavved the cash off Mum for the deposit and the first month's rent, carried my nest into the spare room. The cycle of days revolved as before, only now I had my own bed and lay in it later in the mornings, undisturbed by Ben's prework routine. I stayed up long into the night, playing guitar, chain-smoking, reading.

One of the books I'd snaffled was Coreen's study copy of *The Birth of Tragedy*. It looked like it had been through the washing machine, the dark green cover fading to white at the spine. I tried to read it. Really, I tried. But somehow I never made it past the introduction. I gave up all effort to make sense of it, but kept it by my bedside just the same, like a totem. In the deep of night, when all was silent but for the distant warp of car alarms and the shouts of drunken violence on Brixton Hill, I'd hold that book close and trace her markings, the pages scored with thumbnails, with corners folded back, the underlined words that leapt from the page like a secret message written only for me. *Rausch . . . Schein . . . Das Ur Eine . . .* And that one phrase with its double-underline, almost through to the page beneath:

Tragedy consoles us and seduces us to continue to live.

More my speed were the F. Scott Fitzgerald novels Coreen left lying around. They spoke to me directly, as though reading from the pages of my very own heart. All that yearning, all that aching in silence, the unbridgeable distance between lovers who were meant to—but could not—be. There was something in all of that for me back then.

I did what I could to keep my feelings hidden, but I had to do something with all that pent up longing, and soon enough it began to weep from my fingers, into the guitar. It was pretty weird at first, singing those songs in the bedroom or on the couch, knowing Coreen was there in the flat and could hear every word. Even if the lyrics were oblique, the ache in my voice, in every note, should have told her how I felt. But if it did and she noticed, she never showed it. Instead, she'd come out and listen in silence while I played. Some days she brought out a poem she'd read or written, and I'd sing it along to whatever I was working on.

No words better expressed the way I felt in those days than "Baby, Leave Your Man." Only *I* never wrote it. The song that would launch my career began as a few lines Coreen scratched out over coffee, an open letter to Zelda Fitzgerald. It fit well with some chords I was playing around with and the melody was just there. The whole thing came together in a matter of minutes. Those words may have meant one thing when first penned by Coreen, but as soon as they were on my tongue, falling from my lips, something changed. The words were the same, but by some treacherous alchemy, the song was transformed, became the quintessence of all I could not say aloud.

Neither of us would have imagined where that song would take me in the years that followed, or how many times and to how many people I would have to sing it. No matter how far I traveled, or how long we were apart, there was that piece of Coreen that traveled with me always, a thorn in my heart that stabbed a little deeper with each encore.

Things with Ben weren't going quite so well. Within a few months he started giving me shit about bills and rent and what have you. By then I'd knocked enough songs into shape for a short set, got a few gigs opening for local alt-country acts. Ben told me he liked the shows, but hedged whenever I asked him to put in a good word at the label. Instead he banged on and on about the money I owed him and when was I going to get a job.

He kicked me out a week before Christmas.

I probably should have seen it coming. He'd been shitty with me for weeks, always irritable, always sniping about this or that. It was like I couldn't do anything right. We didn't go to the pub anymore, and in the flat we barely spoke, barely even made eye contact. The bedroom arguments became louder and more frequent. In the mornings, Coreen was not herself.

One afternoon, Ben came home early from work, just after Coreen had left for the day. He was seething. The gist: grab your things and get the fuck out.

I never found out how Coreen felt about it. The next and last time I ever saw her was at the wedding.

8

He whispers and I do not sleep but fall into darkness and the cold.

My thoughts are not my own, my body a stranger, an alien thing of lichen-rock-dirt of decay-rot-moss. I touch the cold and the spiral of life-death etched in skin. The hollow eyes, a skull, no flesh upon these bones. In the mirror only pallor, a face of shadows and cobwebs and eyes that have seen the death that has no end.

They have stopped knocking. There are no answers here. Only the shadows, the pallor.

I am sick and there is no cure but Him. At night his whispers hush away sleep, tell me I am dead I am his. Why run little bird little soul, he whispers. Frail suffering thing, it is only pain when you turn away when you run. Turn to me little soul and this pain is the gate, the grief of life-death-joy from that dirt you are that makes you one with bliss. The suffering that never dies, the all-life that endures eternal for it is all-death. Run not little soul for you are mine and evermore shall be, for suffering is sweetness and what is life without pain and what is pain without love.

The pain is a cord of sinew and nerve and vein that chokes and binds and pulls me down into him and him into me, his hands upon me the weight of rock. No light can reach the dark places of his touch, the pain that makes me long for the flower of death the child of decay in the womb of my mind. We breathe together the air of tombs and *exhale as one the shiver-chill, the breath of this Place of Bones, the breath of lovers entwined. A bower of briar and thorn-ripped flesh in the ecstasy of eternal decay. He in me and I in him and ever evermore shall be. This twist of meat that rots to moss, the blackened gusts of cold smoke-breath, until we are only the bones. Only the gleaming bones.*

There are no dreams without sleep for I am living the death that never wakes.

9

Dawn broke distant and unreal, a scene viewed through the wrong end of a telescope, sounds that faded in like stars in the black silence. And the warmth. The closeness of bare flesh, of the body curled behind me. The soft breath like a whisper on the back of my neck.

I froze, goosepimpling. In that moment fully awake. The sense of wrongness. The disorientation. The faint smell of charred wood.

There was nobody there.

I reached out behind me, gingerly. The airbed creaked as I moved, the sleeping bag rustled. Outside, rosellas scratched on the tin roof, kookaburras mocked from the gully.

Of course there was nobody there.

I lay back and stared at the ceiling, at the rank twist of flypaper with its litter of ancient corpses. The trees blurred behind mildewed windowpanes, moved by a noiseless wind. I had no memory of putting myself to bed.

I flattened my hand against the sheet where the body had been, where it had *seemed* to be. Just the wash-worn flannel, the cold ridges of the air bed. Just the tailings of a very sweet, very real dream. I closed my eyes, dredged for a feeling, an image, anything that I could hold onto. But it was slipping away. All I found was the spangled blackness and a dull throbbing at my temples.

I rolled out of bed and padded onto the deck, filled a cup with water, drank it down, filled another, washed down two tablets of Panadol. I rummaged for coffee, dug out the stovetop espresso, filled it, sparked the stove. The gas roared. I bent double, coughed until I felt my lungs would bleed, then ripped open a fresh pack of cigs, lit one from the stove and sat down on the edge of the deck.

A warm wind filled the air with whispers. Dry leaves danced and quivered, boughs trembled in slow motion. The eucalypts that clung to the gully's edge swayed with languid, underwater movements. The camp chair was where I'd left it the night before, an empty wine bottle beside it. I remembered my dream and thought of Coreen, reached into my pocket for the picture. But it wasn't there.

Dropping down from the deck, I poked around by the chair, peered over the edge of the gully. But I couldn't see it anywhere. I felt again that sensation of being watched, of eyes boring into me.

The light.

The espresso pot hissed and I startled. I got up to pour the coffee, heart tumbling, lit another cig. The sound of the wind had me on edge, that inescapable white noise like an electric current, prickling my nerves. And the memory of the light.

What had happened to the light? I remembered seeing it down in the gully, dancing through the forest, searching—

A lamp? Had there been someone with a lamp down there? The light had been moving toward me. And then?

I couldn't bear to think who might be down there, but not knowing was worse. I sipped at the coffee, stared down into the gully. Treetops bowed in the eerie wind. The swishing of the leaves was like static.

I packed matches, water and Panadol into a canvas bag, ate a tin of cold sweetcorn, drank another coffee, smoked another cig. I flicked through a newspaper half-a-decade out of date. When I was all out of distractions, I picked up the bag and strode down into the gully.

The descent from the train was easy at first, easier still with the wind behind me, urging me forward, downward. I followed the fence-line, stepping carefully through the tussocks and over rotting deadfall, anxious not to touch or disturb any biting, stinging thing that might hang in translucent webs or coil in shadowed spaces. The walk must have stirred up a hangover, as my heart was tripping over itself and my ears were ringing like tinnitus. When the path turned back into the forest, the dry leaves shushed above me like a warning.

I looked back up toward the train and could still just see the tip of the corrugated iron roof. I tried to work out where I was, and where it was I'd seen the light. I hadn't given much thought to what I was actually looking for, and even less to what I might find, what the consequences of that might be. What thoughts I had were vague and half-formed, inchoate impressions of some fearful thing, made worse by my worsening state. With each step the pinprick of discomfort behind my eyes tightened, the ringing in my ears grew louder.

The landscape was changing around me. Murmuring leaves and lush grasses became the gray bones of dead trees, a graveyard of fallen limbs, flesh-colored trunks bleeding sap. I got distracted and strayed from the path, followed a dusty wombat trail.

I stopped for breath, resting beside the skeleton of a fallen tree, tried to work out where I was. But the pain in my head made it hard to think.

The track led down into a fold in the gully side and appeared to come up the other bank, curving around and back toward the train. It might once have been a creek, but there was no sound of water, only the hissing leaves, the whine in my middle ear. I thought about turning around, going back the way I'd come, but I knew what lay behind me and the thought of retracing all those uphill steps made my lungs burn. Going forward there was at least a chance it would be easier. And that I might find whatever it was I was looking for.

Clambering down into the creek bed, I knew I'd made the

wrong choice. It was rocky and unstable, littered with deadfall, snarled with wild blackberry vines. The path disappeared beneath that tangle and to get across I had to veer farther and farther from the track, picking foot- and handholds that wouldn't snap beneath my weight, or snag my clothes or skin on thorns.

By the time I'd made it to the bottom, I had no idea where I'd come down from or where I'd been aiming. I think I started to sob, for the pain was now so bad that the light hurt my eyes and the ringing in my ears had swelled to a roar and I was lost and despairing and all I wanted was to be back in bed with the covers pulled up over my head. But to get there I had to keep going. So I put one foot in front of the other, choosing carefully where I placed my steps, what I held for support.

Down in the creek bed, it was still and dim. The high steep banks shut out all sunlight. Cold seeped from the rocks. The air was dank and fetid and smelled weird, like moss and rot and old burned wood. I saw a rockfall below and made for it, hoping I could use it to scramble out, to curve back up to the train.

The bank ahead had collapsed and the creek bed opened out to form a low amphitheater, a basin of heaped rocks with a mound at the center. Around the edge, three, four, five giant boulders loomed like sentinels. Above, a jury of lifeless trees, bone-gray and coal-black. I clambered over rocks encrusted with lichen, heading toward the far edge where the climb seemed shallowest. I was almost at the base of the mound when I noticed the first heap of bones.

It might once have been a kangaroo; the long bones of the feet and tail, the ribs, the skull, still held a structure that was recognizable, characteristic even. There was no trace of rot, of flesh or fur, only a dull gleam in the murky half-light.

Looking up, I noticed other heaps standing out against the bleak mound. Bones of creatures as small as squirrels and those the size and shape of pigs. Skeletons of birds, of rodents, of reptiles, the hollow carapaces of beetles, cockroaches, cicadas. Snake bones that curled between the rocks like delicate, primitive jewelry. Raptor bones with wings outstretched, the feathers a shadow, a memory. In that rancid gloom, the skeletons almost glowed.

The closer I got to the center, the more bones there were, as though the mound were made not from rock but from the remains of many centuries of creatures, crawling over each other to die. From the center of the heap, cold air rippled in waves.

A sense of dread bloomed inside me like spilled ink, an icy darkness that stifled my breath. I wanted only to be away from there, from the cold, from the bones. But I could not move. I heard a rattling, a flapping, saw something flicker near the top of the mound.

It was pinned against the rock, weighed down by a wide, flat lizard skull. It thrashed in the stillness, buffeted by a hidden wind. I reached up, pinched it between my fingers, felt a current of cold electricity shoot up my arm as I plucked it out. The photo had been torn in half.

Coreen looked out at me with her fierce blue eyes.

My nose began to bleed.

10

The timing could not have been worse.

I was finally getting it together: had a place, a job, a band. Though I'd not seen her in two years or more, Coreen was with me always, like a ghost haunting everything I played. In the vibrations of my guitar strings, the crack in my voice, the ache of every harmony. Labels were sniffing around, making all the right noises. I was getting good press for my solo shows, had a double-album's worth of heartbreakers from the Brixton days. Alt-country was *in*. All that bad shit was in the past.

And then it arrived. The invitation.

A posh envelope with my name on it, in a familiar scratchy hand. It was covered in postmarks and redirection notes, addressed to my mum's place, then again to the last pad I'd crashed. I didn't dare open it. So I got proper sloshed.

Inside was a piece of fancy card, with an Art Deco design and gold leaf around the edge. There were words: *Ben and Coreen invite you* . . . I couldn't read any more. I saw I'd missed the RSVP date.

I was glad of all I'd drunk. It dulled to a distant nausea the cold blade twisting in my gut, stifled like a buried metronome the convulsions of my heart. And it made what I did next seem like a good idea. I took a pen, flipped over that fancy card and wrote Coreen a note. It was short—only four words—but they were well chosen and would have made Nietzsche proud. My own little *Wahnbriefe*. Coreen would know what I meant.

It seemed like a good idea, right up until the moment I dropped the card in the postbox. But then there was no turning back.

Did I regret it? Of course I did, but what did it matter? It wasn't as if I was actually going to go. But as the day drew closer, I found myself becoming more and more anxious. I wasn't thinking about it, but it was there just the same. I drank more than usual, smoked until my fingers were yellow, stopped turning up for work. Some days I didn't even get out of bed. Mostly I just lay there, staring at the ceiling. Sometimes I would pick up the guitar, strum a little, sing a little. But it was lifeless. Not music, but ash and bone.

On the morning of the wedding, though, something clicked. It might've been a dream I had, or something—when I woke, I'd made up my mind. It was a conceit, of course, the old cliché of running into church just as the priest says, "Is there any reason . . ." I knew it was bollocks, but I let it carry me along anyway. That tiny delusional hope felt better than the wilderness of despair that stretched in all directions to infinity.

They were married in a registry office in Lewisham. It was a civil ceremony, some friends in a room watching them say their vows, sign a piece of paper. No church, no priest, no "Is there any reason . . ." All this I learned later. I didn't get my shit together in time and arrived just as the last guests were leaving.

The reception was a grand affair with all the trimmings: a seventeenth century lodge on the outskirts of Greenwich, glorious sunshine on immaculate lawns, a burbling stream that tinkled beneath a fairy-tale bridge. On the gravel outside, a string quartet played classical schmaltz. I felt well underdressed, in my cleanest jeans and a new-enough western shirt. Guests were milling, sipping champers, huddling on the lawn in cliques. Everybody was twiddling their thumbs while the photos were taken, half watching the infinite, fractal configurations of the two families. It went on for-bloody-ever. I shuffled between groups of people I half-knew, third-level acquaintances from uni, faces I recognized from the Brixton days, having abortive, less-than-conversations that trailed off when neither of us had anything to say. I gave up pretending to mingle and instead followed the staff around, plucking champagne flutes from passing trays and ditching the empties.

I was proper smashed by the time they called us in to eat. Ben and Coreen stood by the door to the grand hall, welcoming guests one by one as the procession shuffled past. Ben shook hands, Coreen gave polite kisses. All manner of smiles and hugs and good will gushed from the fawning guests. It reeked of falsehood. I couldn't imagine this to be anything like what Coreen—*my* Coreen—would have wanted. As I got closer, I grew sick to my stomach, like I'd swallowed a ball of lead. I was desperate for a cig and my hands were shaking. I felt like I was falling to pieces.

Ben greeted me first. He had an expression of benevolent reserve, tempered with something that might have been sadness. "Glad you could make it, mate," he said, before turning to greet the person behind me.

Coreen looked drop-dead—pure Jazz Age. She wore a silver-beaded flapper dress and long ivory gloves. Her hair was cut short, straight bangs over an ear-length bob, all held in place with a rhinestone headpiece. She frowned, embraced me formally. I thought I would die. She kissed me on the cheek and her scent lit up inside my skull, tingled up and down my spine and crackled in every nerve; a perfume of soft warmth, of clean sheets and breakfast in bed. The scent of my utter despair.

I wanted to turn and run, to burst out of those grand doors and tear up the gravel, to lumber across the lawn like a hunchback, jump off that fairy-tale bridge and smash my head open on the rocks. But I was so stunned I just let the waitress lead me into the hall, over to a table in the farthest corner.

The meal, when it came, looked delicious. But I couldn't eat a bite. Instead, I drank, ignoring the looks of polite disapproval from the waiting staff whenever I gestured to top up my glass. As the speeches droned on and on, I felt the room spin. I stumbled to my feet, reeled across the hall, barely made it to the gents in time. I passed out, locked in a cubicle with my head on the toilet seat, the bowl spangled with red wine, champagne and stomach acid.

When I came to, my head felt tight as a raisin and the taste of chuck burned in my mouth. I staggered into the corridor. The disco had started and dots of colored light scoured the dark hall where guests whooped and wiggled to the "Time Warp." I stepped out, into the night air, into the smell of summer grass, the sounds of trickling water and distant traffic. Behind me the disco, muffled to a thumping heartbeat.

"Hello, stranger."

Coreen stood beneath the bay windows, just out of the light that spilled across the gravel in geometric patterns. In the darkness, her hair was like an absence, but the beads of her dress and the cut glass in her headband shone, glistering like the scales of a fish. She held her gloves in one hand and a cig in the other, her arm upraised like some careless benediction. She exhaled skyward and the smoke plumed from her lower lip, up and out into the still night.

My stomach lurched. As I steered toward her, she shook a cig from the pack and offered it to me, lit it when I leaned forward. We stood in silence, blowing smoke, staring over at the bridge, the brook, across the silent black lawn.

"So..." I said.

"Yep," said Coreen. "So."

"Coreen..." I began.

"Why don't we just cut the shit," she said, turning to face me. "I got your note."

I drew hard on the cig, looked down at my shoes.

"What the fuck, Jude? What were you thinking? What did you think was going to happen?"

"I thought . . . I mean . . . I don't know. I—"

"Was I supposed to just swoon in your arms, to throw myself at you 'cause you phoned in a love letter on the back of my fucking wedding invitation? *'He said the magic words: now I am his!'* It's my fucking *wedding*, Jude; or did you miss that detail? Or maybe you thought I'm only marrying him 'cause I'd given up waiting for your declaration of . . . of whatever this is."

"Coreen, I . . ."

"You what?"

"I . . ."

"Out with it, Jude. You love me? Not so easy to say now, hey? Not when I'm standing right here. Fuck, Jude. You don't even know me. You don't have the first faintest fucking clue about me, or about Ben, or anyone, because all you give a shit about is yourself."

She flicked the cigarette into the gravel, twisted it beneath her white pump. "I like you, Jude, but you're a real prick, you know. A real selfish prick."

I didn't know what to say. And even if I had known, I couldn't speak—the urge to sob was pushing up from my chest, and my throat ached like I'd swallowed a marble. I just stood there, too heavy to even lift the cig to my lips.

Coreen let out a big sigh, looked back up at me and frowned, shook her head. "Look, I'm sorry," she said. "I didn't mean for it to all come out like that. I've just been stewing on that shit a while. 'Ariadne.' Fuck."

I looked up and, for a moment, our eyes met. I must have looked hurt, or hopeful, or something, because she laughed, frowned that extra-deep frown I knew to be a smile.

"Tell you what," she said, "let's forget it. Let's forget it ever happened, any of it. We'll pretend we're just a couple of old friends having a smoke, talking about the weather. You can take my arm and we'll go back inside and do whatever old friends do at these things. Be happy or something. Get in there and do the Time Warp. Kick that DJ to fucking death."

She pulled her gloves up past her elbows, held her arm out for me. I smiled in spite of myself, nodded, but didn't take it.

"Thanks," I said. "I just need a minute."

"You will come in, won't you?"

"Of course, I'll be in soon. I promise."

She arched her brow and frowned, but nodded, shrugged, then turned and walked back up the steps into the lodge. For a moment, she was silhouetted in the yellowish light from the doorway, a gilt shadow sparkling on the threshold.

That was the last time I ever saw her. As soon as she was out of sight, I turned away from the lodge, the guests, the shit-awful music, turned away from Coreen, and began the long walk home.

01

Sunlight clawed at my eyelids. It burned.

My head *hurt*.

I was curled on the air bed, back in the train. The patina of mold on the carriage windows was aglow, an arcane language written in fire. The sun was low behind the trees and for a moment I lost my bearings. It was in the wrong place. Or was it morning? I'd lost an afternoon and a night.

I tried to remember how I got back here, but it hurt to think; the memories were like Polaroids in a blackout, disconnected flashes with no context. I remembered running, snagged by brambles, clothes and skin tugged and scratched by thorns. Scrambling over rocks, tearing through bushes, tripping along wombat trails to get away from the cold, the smell. And the bones. Dread, like ice, a frozen blackness deep in my chest, propelling me . . . anywhere. Just *away*. Knowing it was madness but running anyway, lungs bursting, head splitting, unable to explain why I ran, or what possessed me. Running with my head tipped back, blood streaming from my nose.

I reached up to my face. My finger came away speckled with flecks the color of rust. The front of my shirt was dark, caked with dried blood.

I pushed myself upright, but the ache in my head spiked, forced me back down. I lay there, head spinning, the pain like corkscrews, like some brutish medieval torture. Hugging my legs tighter to my chest, I burrowed under the covers, tried to block out the sunlight that jagged even through closed eyes.

It was hot inside that sleeping bag, and suffocating, but anything was better than the light and the pain. Maybe I had a fever—my body was burning and yet ripples of cold danced on my skin like arctic breaths. I curled tighter, shivering. Half awake, half delirious, I slipped in and out of consciousness, seeing things, dreaming, yet never quite asleep. I saw the mound of bones and I saw the photo of Coreen, saw it flap crazily in the wind that was not there. Convulsing almost. As though it were alive.

Coreen was gone. She was really gone.

I fell, into darkness, into cold. And all about me, looping like some terrible mantra, the chorus of "Baby, Leave Your Man."

The dream changed and I landed, entombed, buried beneath a mound of rock. I smelled old burnt wood, and moss and lichen and the dampness of rot and dark places. Beneath me, I could still feel the bed, the covers, but above I saw looming boulders, burnt trees, skeletal fingers pointing an accusation at the sky. And everywhere the bones. The pain in my head was so great that I lost all sense of my body, felt myself floating, a waking dream-spirit rising up and over the place of bones.

Below me the patterns coalesced. What had seemed random from the ground became a geometric structure, circles within circles, lines pointing inward, and a spiral of bones that coiled about the center. It began to spin, or I did; the curving trail of bones revolving, whirling, spiraling out toward the edge of the circle. And, as it spun, the bones took shape, animal skeletons reforming, jerked backward, out away from the center. They decayed in reverse. Putrefying flesh grew like lichen on the gleaming bones; swarms of flies rebirthed as writhing maggots; muscles vomited, throbbing and glistening, onto animal architecture. Hearts beat and lidless eyes rolled as the bodies danced from death to life, flickering forward–back, like pictures in a zoetrope.

I felt myself drawn up and up, away from the center. As I withdrew—never sure if it was the place of bones that receded, or me—the cold around me increased. And the darkness.

The spiral of bones became a great arcing stream of animals, sparks on a Catherine wheel of life-death, engulfed, as I pulled back, by the infinite, oceanic blackness. That ball of blue-white light danced, dwindling to a marble, a pea, a pinprick. Until there was only the cold and the dark.

And, in the cold and the dark, I awoke.

It was night. I was shivering, hungry, huddled beneath the covers like an infant in a corpse-womb. The sheets felt moist, but might just have been cold. I was dizzy and my mouth was dry, but my headache had withdrawn to a dull throb that beat time with the ache in my heart. I had no idea *when* I was. I might have slept through the whole of the day, or the morning itself might have been a dream.

I could see the black limbs of trees outside, silhouetted against the blue-black of night, edged with silver from the rising moon. I heard a movement from the corner of the train and froze.

There was a laugh. Then a familiar voice spoke.

"Hey, Country Joe," it said. "Spill.

"Tell me what you're thinking."

12

"Fuck, that didn't come out right. What I mean is, the last months—they took a toll on all of us."

Ben looked more tired than I'd ever known him. I noticed for the first time how haggard he seemed, as though he had, just that moment, let drop the mask of good humor, of competence and stability, and now teetered on the edge of a fall without end.

"It was like living in a nightmare. For me and the girls, but for Coreen most of all. She'd wake up screaming, freaking that someone was in the house, or in our room."

It was late and we were both slumped, in that silence that comes to old houses and backstreet neighborhoods past midnight. I'd been prone on the couch since the girls had gone to bed, and Ben was sinking deeper and deeper into the shadows of the easy chair, barely outlined by the soft glow of the standing lamp. The whiskey he'd brought out was two-thirds gone and had awoken a deep melancholy. The whiskey and the talk of Coreen.

"I'd have to get up, turn all the lights on, go through each room—waking the girls even—just to prove that she was safe, that no one was there. But it wouldn't calm her. I'd wake sometimes to find her sat up, hugging her knees, tearing at the blanket with her teeth. She'd be shivering, like she was cold, even on warm nights. She thought someone was following her, trying to get inside her head."

I'd been waiting for a break in the conversation to duck outside for a cig, but the moment had passed. Ben flashed me an odd look when I lit up and tapped ash into my wine glass.

"It was bad, but alarm bells didn't ring. It wasn't the first time she'd gone . . . *dark* like that. In Margot's first year Coreen went through a real black patch, thought of suicide, all of that. We'd just moved to Oz, I was out all hours for work, and Margot was—she was different. Unresponsive, I suppose. Coreen was alone with this kid who didn't do any of the things that babies are supposed to do—didn't smile, didn't bond—and she lost it. Postnatal depression, the doctor said. We'd always wanted kids, but I don't think either of us really took on how hard it would be, on Coreen most of all. She was a good mum, but it didn't come natural. She really had to work at it.

"When she started forgetting things—lunches for the kids, packing their bags, small stuff—I thought she was just distracted, just going a bit dark again. But then I got a call from the grandparents: could I come and get the girls? Coreen hadn't picked the kids up from school and nobody knew where she was. Her mobile went straight to voicemail and the home phone rang off the hook. We found her in the bedroom. She'd locked herself in, pushed a dresser in front of the door. Paper was everywhere, like someone had emptied out a filing cabinet. She'd been making notes."

"She was writing again?"

"Not exactly—it was crazy stuff. Full-on fucked-up lunatic stuff. But I humored her, you know. I thought she was trying to work it all out, that it would be good to let her get it out of her system. Catharsis, or whatever. But it didn't help, just made things worse. I tried to pick up the papers, to clear some space so we could go to bed, but she freaked, turned on me—*growled* at me. She wouldn't let me in the bed after that. I slept with Peg.

"I had to keep the girls away from her because she frightened them, and I was afraid of what she might do. She was making no sense, acting . . . She acted like she was insane. I wanted her to see someone—anyone—who could help her get over these crazy feelings, this madness that kept her awake all night, shut her up all day. But she wouldn't leave the room, wouldn't talk, wouldn't eat. Just locked herself away to scribble those fucking notes. She looked like a skeleton, her skin was so pale you could see through it, and her hair had gone to dreads. When I went in to check on her, she'd jump out of her skin, stare at me with her eyes bulging, like I was coming to kill her, like she didn't know who I was even.

"I thought it was just some kind of breakdown, a manic phase. I kept telling myself it would pass."

"But it didn't?"

"It didn't. It just went on and on. And the deeper into it we got, the harder it was to do anything about it, like we'd left it too late to help her. Her mum wanted me to have her committed, made an appointment for me to see some headshrinker. But then Coreen had the seizure."

Ben stooped for the whiskey, filled his glass to brimming then capped the bottle, tossed it over. He drained half the glass in a gulp, lay back with his eyes closed for an age. I thought he must have passed out, but then I saw the hand clutching the glass was shaking. He knocked the rest back in one.

"I was putting Peg to bed. She was three, three-and-a-half then— just little. We were sat up reading a story, about a bear who's lost his hat." He laughed without humor. "Funny what you remember. There was this crash from the bedroom, then thumping. I jumped up and ran to the door, but it wouldn't open. I charged it, figured she'd put the dresser there again. But it was her. She'd collapsed beside the bed, having a fit. Her elbow was banging and banging against the cupboard, head snapping back and forward. She was foaming."

I wanted to say something, but there was nothing *to* say. Ben was lost, sinking, as the recollection gained momentum.

"I yelled at Margot to call an ambulance. Peg was in the doorway crying. I was trying to find something to put in Coreen's mouth—how they always say to put something in their mouth, so they don't bite off their tongue. I didn't know what was happening. I thought she was dying."

I lit another cig. Ben gestured and I tossed him the pack, the lighter. He hadn't smoked since the Brixton days, so it was weird to see him spark one; fingers out, thumb up, like a make-believe pistol. We sat in silence while Ben smoked. His mouth was twisted.

"I rode with her in the ambulance. They gave her some drug to calm her down, to stop the seizure. But, when she came to at the hospital, she was paralyzed all down her left side. They took her off to be scanned, found the tumor. It was big as a golf ball. On the screen it was like this black hole in a ring of white fire, like she was burning up inside.

"The doctors told me it'd be fine, that they'd operate in a week, two at most, that I should go home, get some rest. It made no sense. How could she be fine? How could you lose that much of yourself, of your brain, and still *be*?

"Not long after I'd gone, she had another fit. She fell unconscious and they dragged her off to surgery, called me back in. I thought that was it, that I was never going to see her again."

"And she . . . ?"

"It was fine. I mean, it was fucked—the waiting, not knowing. But when she came out of it, there she was. Same old Coreen. Pale as hell, looking like death, looking like some Celtic witch with one side of her head all shaved. But she smiled when she saw me and I knew it was her, that we had her back."

Ben looked at the cigarette in his hand, as though surprised to find it there. It had burned down to the filter, leaving a tower of ash. He dropped it in his whiskey glass.

"It was her, and it wasn't. The madness, the fear, *that* had all been cut away with the tumor. But the Coreen we brought home was not the woman I married. She was placid, docile even. She knew us, me, the kids. But something was gone.

"She wanted me to tell her about it, everything that had happened. She'd lost months, was blank all the way back to our last holiday, down at the train. I remembered then how she'd been laid up that week with a migraine, how she woke us all up one night with this dreadful wailing. That was the first of the nightmares."

"And what about the notes?"

"I trashed them. There was nothing there but crazy talk, fucking mind-babble. I wanted to put it behind us, not have her go back and wallow in it all over again. I was afraid of what that might do to her.

"In the end, it made no difference. A month later, she had another attack and died before we made it to the hospital."

We sat in silence. Ben stared down at his hands.

"Ben, I . . ."

"It's okay, I know. I'm just glad you're here. It's been too long, Jude."

I looked down, sparked my last cig, feeling guilty as hell.

"I was wrong, you know," Ben said. He gave a sad smile and nodded to himself. "Pretentious fucking first-year, didn't know what I was bloody on about."

"About . . .?"

"Derrida," he said. "Turns out he fucking loved Nietzsche."

13

"Hello, stranger."

A creeping cold had infiltrated the carriage. My skin prickled, breath pluming like smoke. Time froze, ground to a glacial crawl. My heart had all but stopped.

Silver moonlight filtered impossibly through the carriage windows, drawing dim outlines of furniture from the shadows: the dresser, the wicker chair. Everything was in monochrome. Everything, except Coreen.

Her skin, in the moonlight, seemed to phosphoresce, a cold burning silver broken only by the dark smudge of her mouth, the black pennies of her nipples. There was a faint smell in the carriage, of charred wood, of moist lichen. The chair creaked.

"Aren't you going to say hello?" The words came out, but her lips were still as a photograph. Her mouth was round, expressionless.

"Coreen," I said at last. "You're dead."

"Aren't you pleased to see me, stranger?" Her eyes looked hurt, but still her mouth did not move.

"No," I said. "No, you're dead. You can't be here."

She smiled, her mouth twisting upward into a grimace. "How can I be dead?" As she spoke, she ran her hands up her belly, over her ribcage, cupped and squeezed her breasts. "I'm right here, aren't I? Do I look dead to you?"

I couldn't help but watch, as she ran her hands down her sides, over her hips, her thighs.

She stood in that ghastly light and revealed a landscape of pale incandescence; the twin black coins and the dark island between her legs, abandoned campfires on a beach of white sand. Her hair fell about her shoulders like feathers and her eyes burned black, holding my gaze.

She stepped toward the bed with measured, almost balletic steps, smoothing her body with delicate hands, her thighs, her belly, her breasts. And while the cadaverous twist of her mouth was a wrongness that filled my bowels with horror, her subtle gyrations possessed me, roused the lust I'd held in check so many years.

"I came back for you, stranger," said the unmoving mouth. "I couldn't live without you. I wanted you. Always."

She was beside me now, her black forest just inches from my face. The smell of damp moss overwhelmed me. I was shaking—with terror, with desire.

"What's my name," I managed to whisper. "Tell me my name."

She smiled once more, the upward twist of her mouth like a broken spring. "Why, you're my stranger, of course. My own sweet Country Joe."

She leaned over me, straddled me, pushed down against me.

"And you," I gasped. "What's . . ." I was shaking, weeping with fear. And relief. I couldn't help myself.

I reached out my hands, cupped her breasts, ran them down her sides, around her thighs to the cold ivory of her buttocks, tracing a path they had smoothed many thousands of times in my dreams.

The thing that was not Coreen leaned forward with parted lips and her black tongues slid inside me like lizards. She clamped her mouth over mine and I gave myself to her completely, to the shining silver of her nakedness, to the dark warmth inside her, to the acrid smell of burnt wood and forest rot that leached from her skin, from her pitch-black hair.

I tore off my clothes like a madman, gave myself to the dream, to this moment I had longed for since I first laid eyes on her; that other Coreen in that other world, all those years before.

She pulled me inside and I was lost.

14

cold so cold the breath like ice that gusts down sides of hill so close to top i dare not look from this great height afraid how far there is to fall and all to lose let go would end to pain but worse i fear ahead-behind hand-over-hand up hill of bones drag tired body cobweb-shadow over rough architecture of thousand-animal-dead meat-ribbons red-trailing behind life-white corpse this meat-skeleton crawls onward-upward-toward whatever lies in wait like predator of death-lust lust-death hands raw skin flayed muscle meat and tendons sick-strung bunting on the mound of bone as bone myself i pull what is left up bone-by-bone another heap of bones atop this death-hill dying wind-ice-breath from wide-mouth cracked-lip-ring of falling bones that rattle down that ever-throat a well of blackness-unto-black and foul-gusting life-after-breath the smoke of ruin-decay and ever-pain the mouth of hell down into blackness stare with black-eyes-death-eyes and from that blackness know He comes inhale his breath ache for his touch the black tongues snicker-snake from bone-hill-mouth and twine-tangle round my neck and head and tender-strangle-tug the last that parting lips the muscle-motion penetrates descends sink-searches out my deepest dark his death-kiss-tongue throat-fills to belly-down and surrender he clench-ejects black-passion-blooms inside erupting belly-shadows black-flower-blossom life-light-nectar-essence *wither-desiccate-decays and only-bones-remain clatter-rattle-rain bones-down death-god-worship-hill only-me is him-within-me-within-him-within falling into—*

15

"How long have you been in love with my mother?"

The voice pierced the murk like a light from beyond the grave, tugging at me, pulling me free of that delicious weight of darkness, of whiskey and wine and too little sleep. I had vague memories of Ben saying goodnight, of me saying I'd sit up for just one more drink, and then—

I'd passed out on the couch.

Beneath my head, the folded duvet, the pile of sheets Ben tossed down before he crashed. Digging into my back, the empty bottle of Jamesons. Pressed against the zip of my jeans, an unwelcome, hotly uncomfortable erection.

The standing lamp in the corner still glowed orange, but dirty gray light was seeping through the slatted blind. My eyes were puffed and rancid, like rotten fruits. It hurt to keep them open.

I yawned, coughed, felt around for my cigs, almost died of a heart attack.

Just inches from my face, a gleaming animal skull.

Margot had pulled the pouf up next to the couch and sat there, chin forward, back straight, hands in the lap of her charcoal pinafore. Her eyes were the coldest blue—like ashes or molten silver. Her mouth was twisted into a tight little frown.

"Shit, Margot." I sat up, tugged the duvet over my lap. "You startled me."

"You're in love with her, aren't you?"

"Who are we talking about, Margot? I'm not sure I follow—"

"You're lying," she said, "because you're afraid that Daddy will find out."

She rested the skull in her lap. It looked like a rat, but obscenely big. A capybara, perhaps. Or a wombat. She stroked its forehead with a finger, as though it were a living pet curled up there on her knee.

"I'm not lying," I said, and looked down at my hands. They were clenched into fists. I let them curl open.

"Don't be afraid," she said. "I won't tell."

I looked back at Coreen—at Margot. They were so alike my heart sent out jolts of pain, an alternating current that pulsed now with grief, now with yearning.

"Is it that obvious?"

"Perhaps. Perhaps only to me. Grownups always talk about how I look like her. Daddy, Granny, Grandpa. They stare at me with their sad eyes, like I'm the one who's dead. They pretend they're listening, but I know they're thinking of her, seeing her instead of me." At that she frowned, but her eyes sparkled. "You do it too, though you probably don't know it. Stare at me with that faraway look. Even now you're doing it: looking at me, thinking of her. How *does* that feel, exactly?"

My cheeks burned. I rummaged around the couch, pretending to look for my cigs.

"You must miss her very much," I said.

Margot tilted her head to one side, examined me like a test subject exhibiting some unexpected behavior. Her frown deepened.

"I'm not sorry she's dead, if that's what you mean. Things are easier without her." She paused, and a look of genuine amusement spread across her face. "But not for you."

I found the pack, tapped it against my palm. It was empty.

"It must feel strange," she said. "To have come all this way. For nothing."

I pressed my fingers into my temples, my forehead. A headache was blooming there like blood in a syringe. I closed my eyes.

"You're right," I said. "It is strange."

Margot raised an eyebrow.

"I'm sorry, it's just . . ."

"Don't be sorry," she said. "It doesn't mean anything to me. Or her. What is there to be sorry for?"

"Because I miss her. Because she—"

"Don't be sorry," she said again. "It's not like you killed her."

Margot lifted the skull and, moving its jaw like a puppet, said in a harsh squeak, "That would be *me!*"

"What?" I winced.

"Silly Mummy," Margot continued in the squeaky voice, still waggling the ivory jawbone. "Dragging poor Margot off on a stupid bushwalk when she didn't want to go. But Margot found me and all my lovely friends so that made her happy. Until Mummy got all dizzy and wanted to leave. Margot took me with her but Mummy said, 'Put it back, I'm scared.' But we wanted to stay together so we ran and left Mummy crying in the woods."

"You're not making sense, Margot," I said, rubbing my temples. "Your mother had something wrong with her brain."

Margot lowered the skull, fixed me with her stare like a moth on a pin. "Yes," she said, in her usual, affectless tone. "A tumor, I know. And of course I know I didn't kill her; I'm not superstitious. I'm a scientist. But *she* thought so. She was terrified of all those bones. Quite ridiculous."

"But," I said pointlessly. The wine and whiskey were wreaking their bitter revenge, churning my gut, spinning the room. "What bones? What are you even talking about?"

Margot pulled something from behind her and waved it in front of me. It was a bundle of papers torn from a school pad, black with scratchy handwriting.

"Her madness diary, Daddy called it. He threw it away when Mummy was in hospital, but I took it from the bin. Utter nonsense, of course—completely unscientific."

I reached for the papers, but she tugged them back and I spilled from the couch.

There was a sound from above, like a jackhammer tumbling down the stairs. Margot tossed the pages down in front of her, shook her head as I scrabbled on the floor to gather them together. I slid the sheaf beneath the pile of bedding just as Peg burst into the room. Margot tensed, frowned, straightened her pinafore and walked out. Peg jumped onto the couch beside me, bouncing up and down on her knees.

"Judy, Judy, Judy, Judy! Play a song, Jude! Play me a song!"

"Leave him alone, Peg," said Ben from the door. "I reckon Jude will need a cup of tea before he's human enough for music. How you feeling, mate? We'd better get a feed on before you go. You've got a long drive ahead of you."

16

Through the carriage windows I saw daylight of sorts, an indeterminate twilight of mute gray that could have been dusk, could have been dawn, could have been any London afternoon.

My clothes lay heaped where I'd thrown them, in that moment of fever, of madness.

Coreen was nowhere to be seen.

I put out a hand to touch where she'd been, where she'd fallen asleep beside me as I lay awake, entangled in a briar of contentment and disgust, satiety and horror. The space was rumpled and still warm and I rolled over and pressed my face into it, inhaling the smell of mold and smoke that exuded from her every pore. The aftertaste of her was everywhere, on the bed, on me. I lay back, struggling to contain my frustrated arousal.

I knew it was not her. But I longed for it anyway, for the thing that was not Coreen.

I picked up my cigs from the bedside table, shook one out, put it to my lips. Tobacco dust poured from the end, leaving only the filter and a hollow paper tube. I took another from the pack but the paper crumbled, disintegrated. A cloud of brown powder burst over the sheet. I tried another, the last, but it fell to pieces before I'd pulled it from the pack.

Closing the lid, I tossed the box back down on the table. I didn't feel like smoking anyway. Didn't feel like anything. My headache was entirely gone, and with it my hunger. I had no urge to cough, to clear my throat. I felt . . . nothing. I stood and walked to the nearest window. I was disoriented, but it wasn't anything I could put my finger on. Everything had changed somehow but, when I looked about, I couldn't pinpoint the difference. Whatever it was, it was there, right before me. And yet—

I was naked, but I was not cold. When I exhaled, a silver plume of condensation escaped my lips. There was a layer of white powder encrusted on the inside of the windows, on the surfaces of dressers and cabinets. It looked like dust or ash, but crunched minutely when pressed. It was frost. But I was not cold.

It was then I noticed the silence. True silence. Not just quiet, but a total absence of sound of any kind. I felt panic rise. Had I gone deaf? But when I stopped to listen, I could hear my breath whistle in my nostrils. When I stepped away from the window, I heard the shuffle of my feet on the carpet. And yet, the silence was everywhere.

I walked out onto the deck, feeling the slight prickle of splinters from the boards beneath my feet. It seemed more weathered than I remembered, a little more warped, a little more faded. Dead leaves banked in chaotic drifts against the carriage. The day itself was unlike any I'd ever known, toneless and completely flat. The sky was a dull gray dome, unmarked by cloud or sun. The air, still. The trees along the edge of the gully were motionless, colorless, like an overexposed black-and-white photograph.

As I walked the length of the train, some voice in the back of my mind was babbling that it was not too late, that I'd committed to nothing, that I could still escape this madness. It told me to get in the car, to drive away, to just drive and not stop until I reached the city. I could still find Mack, still make it to the show. The voice told me I could run and leave all of this behind me, a twisted dream that would fade in time.

But even before I saw the car, I knew I would not leave. The wittering of that tiny voice was the only sound in the world, and it was getting smaller with each moment, overwhelmed by the silence that lay over everything like a snowdrift. And the silence was inside me too, a stillness and a quiet that muffled thought, stifled the voice. Soon, even that would fade to a mosquito's whine and nothing would remain to connect me to the world I'd left behind. Coreen was dead, had been dead to me long before the madness or the tumor. The woman I loved had never been Coreen but some idealized composite that did not exist outside my own imagining. Whatever visited me in the carriage last night was as close to the woman I'd loved as Coreen had ever been; closer even, for it knew me to the bottom of my darkest depths, knew things about me even I did not know.

And it wanted me. *Hungered* for me.

The car was not how I remembered. It was parked as I'd left it, but the roof and hood were collapsed, the windscreen filigreed with lichens. One window had shattered and the door below it was streaked with bird shit. Inside, the gutted seats were spangled with glass, impossible anatomies of rusted springs and eucalyptus leaves. The tires had rotted entirely away, leaving blighted wheel hubs and bolts half-buried in the dirt.

How long had I slept?

I looked at my hands, raised them to my head, pulled them down over my face. There was nothing left of me but longing.

I knew then I would do whatever was asked of me, no matter the cost. To be with her I would offer myself up, a sacrifice on the altar of rocks, to whatever god or demon rules over that place of bones. I would lay down in the chill gloom of the amphitheater, upon the hollow bodies of those who'd lain down there before me, and look up at those tortured husks that jag the sky with burnt, accusing limbs. I would give everything, leave nothing but the bones.

Perhaps I'll go there tonight, bobbing among the eucalypts like a blue-white will-o'-the-wisp—if not tonight then tomorrow night, or some other night like it. I will search the darkness for my love, my home, for that place on which I will make the final offering.

If it is not already made.

ABOUT THE AUTHOR

J. Ashley-Smith is a British-Australian writer of dark fiction and other materials. His short stories have twice won national competitions and been shortlisted seven times for Aurealis Awards, winning both Best Horror ("Old Growth," 2017) and Best Fantasy ("The Further Shore," 2018).

J. lives with his wife and two sons in the suburbs of North Canberra, gathering moth dust, tormented by the desolation of telegraph wires.

DID YOU ENJOY THIS BOOK?

If so, word-of-mouth recommendations and online reviews are critical to the success of any book, so we hope you'll tell your friends about it and consider leaving a review at your favorite bookseller's or library's website.

Visit us at www.meerkatpress.com for our full catalog.

Meerkat Press
Asheville